READY READERS

W9-BLJ-266

STAGE 2
GRADES 1-3

Dear Parents:

Children learn to read in stages, and all children develop reading skills at different ages. **Ready Readers™** were created to promote children's interest in reading and to increase their reading skills. **Ready Readers™** stories are written on two levels to accommodate children ranging in age from three through eight. These stages are meant to be used only as a guide.

Stage 1: Preschool—Grade 1

Stage 1 stories have short, simple sentences with large type. They are perfect for children who are getting ready to read or are just becoming familiar with reading on their own.

Stage 2: Grades 1—3

Stage 2 stories have longer sentences and are a bit more complex. They are suitable for children who are able to read but still may need help.

All of the **Ready Readers™** stories are fun, easy-to-follow tales that are colorfully illustrated. Reading will become an exciting adventure. Soon your child will not only be ready, but eager to read.

Educational Consultant, Shereen Gertel Rutman, M.S.

CONTENTS

Friends Around the World

Illustrated by Sue Mills

Meg Goat was in her school Talent Show.
She won the grand prize.
She won a trip around the
world!

"You did a great job, Meg," Mrs. Goat
said proudly.
"Let's go pack, Mom," said Meg.

Meg left her home in Switzerland.
Her first stop was China. She met Scott
Panda.

"I'll show you around China," said Scott.

Later, they had a wonderful dinner. After dinner, Meg had to leave.

"Thank you for the great visit," said Meg.

"Write me a letter soon," called Scott.

Meg's next stop was Australia. Mark Kangaroo was her guide.

"Welcome to my home," Mark said. "There are so many great places to see."

"Hop in my mother's pouch," called Mark. "She will give you a ride!"

Later that day, it was time to say good-bye. Meg and Mark promised to keep in touch.

Their next stop was Antarctica. Liz Penguin
was there to greet Meg and Mrs. Goat.
"Dress warmly," Liz warned them. "It gets
very cold here!"

Meg had never seen so much ice and snow.

"It's time for me to leave," Meg said sadly.

"I wrote a letter already and you haven't even left!" laughed Liz.

Meg was having so much fun. She made
so many new friends!

The next stop was the United States.

"Welcome to Yellowstone National Park," said Bart Buck.

Bart showed Meg trees, lakes, and animals.

"Thanks for sharing your home," Meg said to her new friend.

Soon, Meg was off to another place.
"Welcome to Peru," said a voice nearby.
"I'm Patti Llama and I'll show you around."

Patti led Meg and her mother through the rain forest. Soon, it was time for Meg to leave.

"Have a safe trip home," Patti said.

Meg's last stop was Africa.

"Welcome to the Nile River Valley," said Jacob Crocodile.

"It is really hot here," Meg replied. "It is much different than Antarctica!"

Jacob Crocodile was an outstanding tour guide. After a camel ride, it was time to go. "I'll write to you soon," promised Meg.

Soon, Meg was back home. She was
happy to see her friends and family again.

Meg missed her new friends. She wished that her new friends could meet each other.

"I'll write to my new friends now," Meg said.

Mrs. Goat gave Meg some pretty paper.
"I'm going to tell each of my new friends
about the others," Meg said.

"I miss you all so much," Meg wrote. "I wish you could come and visit me. I wish you could meet each other."

Soon, Meg received letters from Mark, Scott, Liz, Bart, Patti, and Jacob. They were all coming to visit her at the same time!

Meg was so excited! She showed them the Alps. They played games. Everybody had lots of fun.

"You're a great guide, Meg," Bart said.

One evening, they went camping. They took turns telling about their countries.

One day, they had a picnic. Liz Penguin was very happy. She did not have to wear a coat or hat!

Soon it was time for everyone to leave.
Meg made a special list. The list had
everyone's address and phone number on it.

Everyone got a copy. Now, they could all keep in touch!

At the airport, everyone thanked Meg for helping them meet each other.

"Next time you can all come and visit me!" said Jacob.

They were so happy. They had friends from around the world!

Smiling Sam's Joke Plan

Illustrated by Toledo and DiGregorio Design

Smiling Sam went for a walk. Smiling Sam carried his son, Zeke. Fluffy the cat and Spot the dog took a walk, too.

Smiling Sam stood on his head.
He picked apples with his toes.
Everyone laughed.
   "What shoes are made
from bananas?" Sam asked.

"Tell us!" Zeke said.
"Slippers!" Sam yelled.

Smiling Sam went to see
Mrs. Green.

"King Al made a new law," said Mrs.
Green. "We cannot laugh or smile. The king
locked my husband in a cell!"

41

The grown-ups talked. The children danced. The children played.

Sam thought. Then Sam smiled.
"I will make the king change
his mind," said Sam.

Then Sam asked a question.
"How are a skunk and a pail of milk different?"
"I don't know," Mrs. Green said.

"Then I won't ask you to milk a
cow!" laughed Sam.

Sam and Zeke set off for the palace.
Fluffy and Spot went too.

They saw an old man.

"Listen, listen to the news," the man shouted. "The king is locking people up. Do not smile. You will be locked in a cell."

"Don't worry," said Sam.

"What food makes good music?" Sam asked.
"I don't know," said the man.
"A beet!" laughed Sam.

Smiling Sam got to the palace. Everyone looked very sad.

Zeke said, "Look at that sad girl! Look at the animals. They are sad, too."

53

"You better not smile," said an old dog.
"You could be locked up!"
"Why is it against the law to smile?"
asked Sam.

"It was terrible," said the old dog. "King Al's daughter got married. He told jokes at the wedding. No one laughed. Then Mr. Green snored. The king locked him in a cell!"

Sam went to the palace.
"May I talk with the king?" Sam asked.
Sam asked about the new law.

Sam told the king his plan.

"I will send you seven jokes each week. Tell one joke each day. If people laugh, set Mr. Green free. If no one laughs, put me in jail."

"You must be very sure of yourself. You must think that you are smart. You are brave," said the king. "So be it. There is no law about laughing."

On Monday, King Al asked a joke.
"What do hungry ducks eat?"
No one answered.
"Quackers!" shouted the king.

Everyone laughed. The king laughed, too.
He danced all around.

"Free Mr. Green!" King Al cried. "Now everyone can tell jokes!"

Everyone clapped. Everyone sang and danced. Everyone could tell jokes. Thanks to Smiling Sam's plan!

The Rabbit Brothers Plan Ahead

Illustrated by Robert Sabuda

Rick, Ray, Ryan, and Reese are brothers. They all look alike. They are all eight years old. They all have the same birthday. Even their rooms look the same—messy!

They seem a lot alike. But some things are different. Each brother wants to do something different. Each wants a different job.

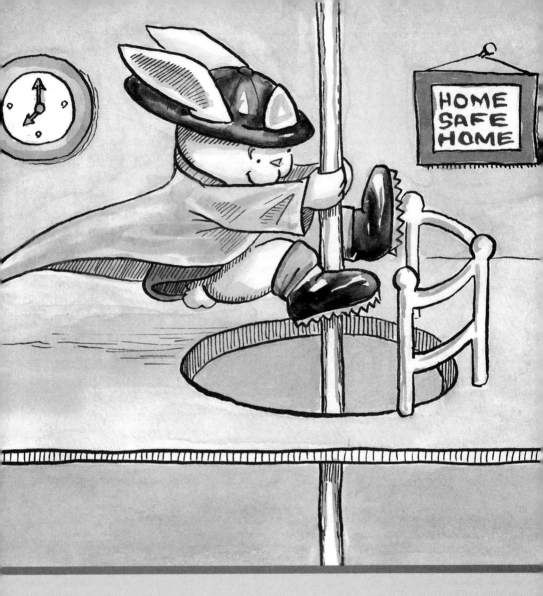

"I will be a firefighter when I grow up,"
says Rick. "I will wear a fire hat, a fire coat,
and boots. I will slide down the fire pole."

"I will ride a red fire truck," Rick shouts.

"I will race to a fire," says Rick.

"I will be very careful," he says.

"I will climb a tall ladder," says Rick.

"I can save a kitten in a tree!" he cries.

The brothers like the idea. But Ray has a different plan.

"I will be the captain of a boat," Ray says.
"I will sail the seas. I will take a different
trip every day."

"The water may be bumpy. I will save the big boats," Ray says.

"My boat will help other boats. A boat can lose its way," he says. "My boat will be very strong."

"My job will be fun," Ray says.

"I can race my boat with a whale!"

The brothers like that idea, too. But Ryan has a different plan.

"I want to fly a magic rug!" Ryan says.
"I can use the rug from my room."

"My magic rug will fly high in the sky. I will fly near the clouds. I will fly near the birds," says Ryan.

"I will do cool tricks!" he says.

"At night I will fly into space," Ryan says.

"I will fly near the stars!"

"I will fly to the moon," Ryan says. "I will see the man in the moon. He will blow at my rug! I will hold on tight!"

The brothers like the idea. But Reese has a different plan.
"I want to fly," says Reese.

"I will fly high in the sky," says Reese. "I will fly over mountains and trees."

"I will fly over the sea," says Reese.

"I will wave to everyone on the ground."

"When the wind blows, I will be brave. I will be strong," says Reese.

"I will not be afraid," he says. "I will land safely on the ground."

The brothers like the idea. So does Mrs. Rabbit. But she has a different plan. She tells Rick, Ray, Ryan, and Reese her plan. They must clean their rooms before supper!

Magic Island

This is Magic Island. It is a special place.

Walt Witch is the ruler of the good kingdom. His part of the island is peaceful. It is a happy place.

Witch Stony is the ruler of
the evil kingdom. His part
of the island is scary. It is
a dark place.

Many magical creatures live near Walt Witch. None of the creatures like to live near Stony. He takes away the creatures' magical powers.

Unicorns live on Magic Island. They are special creatures. They are the most magical creatures on the island.

Stony wants all of the magic power. He wants to get rid of all of the good magic. He made a spell that turned the unicorns into stone. Only one unicorn escaped this spell.

Mandy is the last unicorn on Magic Island. Without her, the good magic would be gone forever. Then Stony would be in power.

Princess Kari protects Mandy from Stony. Princess Kari dreams of becoming a good witch. She wants to break Stony's spell. She wants to free all of the other unicorns.

"Please teach me to be a witch," Princess Kari begged.

"In time, my dear. You are still too young," Walt Witch replied.

Kari was sad. She wanted to stop Stony.

Mandy hopes that Princess Kari can stop Stony.

"It won't be long until Stony's spell is broken!" says Mandy to the stone unicorns.

"Princess Kari must never beat me!" said Stony.

He came up with a plan. He called on his evil pets, Hex and Rex. They would help him trick the princess.

Hex and Rex waited for Princess Kari.

"Do you want to free the unicorns?" asked Hex.

"Follow us. We know where Stony keeps his spell book," said Rex.

Kari jumped for joy. She could break the spell if she had Stony's spell book!

Hex and Rex tricked the princess. Once Kari was gone, Stony's helper, Les, captured Mandy!

Princess Kari knew that Stony tricked her!
She asked all her friends to help save
Mandy.
"Don't worry, we'll save
her," said Brendan Dragon.

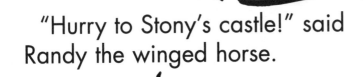

"Hurry to Stony's castle!" said
Randy the winged horse.

Stony made a poison drink. He went to give Mandy the drink. But it was too late! Mandy's friends were at the door. Stony spilled the poison drink on himself and his pets! They all turned to stone!

"I'm glad you're safe, Mandy," said Princess Kari.

Now Princess Kari knew Stony's spell. She was able to free the unicorns. Walt Witch taught Kari to be a great and kind witch. Everyone was happy. They were no longer afraid of Stony. Stony was gone. Now the magic on Magic Island would last forever.

But Stony and his pets weren't really gone. They were used to decorate Magic Island!

Bailey's Surprise

Illustrated by M. Cambraia Magalhaes

Eve Woodpecker knocked
on Bailey Bunny's door.
"I know a secret. You must promise
not to tell," warned Eve.

Bailey promised. Eve told him about
a surprise party for Jill Squirrel. Jill lived in
Forest Village. Bailey was excited. He loved
surprises! He loved parties!

On the train to Forest Village, they saw Chris.

"Hi Chris," said Bailey. "Are you coming to Jill's party?"

"Bailey, that's a secret!" exclaimed Eve.

"Oh, I forgot," Bailey said.

Bailey and Eve arrived in Forest Village. Bailey saw his friend, Kyle. He told Kyle about the party.

Everyone nearby heard him.

"That's great," said Mr. Fox. "I can't wait!"

"I'm sorry," said Bailey to Eve. "I didn't mean to tell them about the party."

"That's okay, but no more mistakes," said Eve. "We don't want Jill to find out!"

The next day, Bailey and Eve visited
Viv Beaver. They painted toys that
Viv carved.

"Jill will love this boat," Bailey said.
"I will give it to her at her surprise party."

"What surprise party?" asked Viv.

"Oops," gulped Bailey.

"That's the third time you've told someone. Jill will surely find out!" Eve shouted.
"I'm sorry," Bailey said sadly.

Next, Bailey and Eve visited Mrs. Hen's
school. Bailey told everyone there about the
surprise party.

"Just don't tell anyone," said Bailey.

Mrs. Hen and the children waved
good-bye.
"Don't worry, we will keep your secret!"
said Mrs. Hen.

The next morning Bailey saw some
of his friends.

"Hi Bailey," yelled Fred Monkey.

"We're going to play a game,"
said Sal Puppy.

"I know a secret," said Bailey. "I'm not supposed to tell."

"Please tell us," said Sammie Peacock.

Bailey told them all about the party.

Finally, the big day came. Bailey was very surprised. Jill Squirrel was already there.

"SURPRISE!" everyone shouted.

Bailey was confused.

"The party is really for you," said Jill. "We told you a fake story. We didn't want you to know the truth!"

Eve told Bailey about the party.
"Everyone knew about it," she bragged.

"It was hard to pretend not to know," said Viv.

"I think I kept the secret best," Fred said.

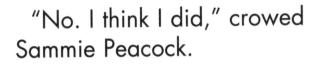

"No. I think I did," crowed Sammie Peacock.

"It's hard to keep a secret—that is if your name is Bailey!" said Paul Lion.

151

Bailey was so excited and surprised.
Jill made all of Bailey's favorite foods.
All of Bailey's friends were there. It was
a great party!

The next day Bailey and Eve went home.
"Next year, I will throw a surprise party
for you," Bailey said.
"That's if you can keep
the secret!" laughed
Eve.

TRAIN

STATION

The Greatest Treasure

Illustrated
by
Fran Rizzo

Justin and his sister Kate live on a ship. They go on adventures. Some of their friends are Lucky and Trixie Duck, Cal Cat, and Peppy Parrot.

Justin uses his telescope. Look! There's
Ethan Octopus.

Justin likes to jog with Ethan. It's hard to keep up. Justin only has two legs!

One day, Kate and Justin wanted to search for treasure. Trixie, Lucky, and Cal wanted to search, too.

They searched high and low. They searched the beach, the hills, and the valleys.

"I don't think we'll find any fortune," Justin said.

"We'll find something," said Kate.

While she was searching, Kate saw the Turtle family. Tyler, Tess, and Trevor Turtle were great pals.

Kate knew that there was no fortune on this part of the island. They must search someplace else.

They walked for a while. They reached trees and mountains. Suddenly, Kate saw a trail of footprints. Everyone was happy.

"Where do you think the trail leads?"
Peppy Parrot asked.
  "I hope it leads to hidden fortunes,"
said Justin.

"Maybe we'll find a giant chest filled with fun prizes," hoped Kate.

"I could use a new telescope," said Justin.

"I want new sunglasses," Trixie Duck said.

"I want a new ball of yarn!" exclaimed Cal.

They finally got to the end of the trail. They were surprised by what they found. There was a farm!

"Maybe there is fortune hidden there!" Kate said.

They crept a bit closer. Then they saw a funny sight. There were animals singing and dancing.

"Hi," said a little girl. "I'm Julie. This is my brother Bobby."

"Welcome," said Bobby. "You're just in time for our party!"

Justin and Kate watched a strange band play music.

Lenny the donkey played the drums. He was great.

Susie the goat was on the guitar.

Marvin the horse played beautiful tunes.

Michelle Mouse's instrument was bigger than her whole body!

The mule brothers, Hank and Milo, made music on their pipes.

Nikki the parrot pounded the piano.

Four ducks, Duke, Dan, Darren, and Dave, sang songs.

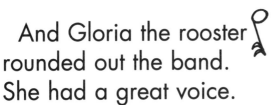

And Gloria the rooster rounded out the band. She had a great voice.

There was dancing, too.

The kittens, Cara, Sara, and Kira, danced the can-can.

Gracie the pig danced high on her toes.

Tony the turtle tap-danced to the music.

After the wonderful show, everyone had ice cream.
"Who wants more?" Julie asked.

Justin and Kate didn't want the fun to end. But it was getting late.

"I guess it's time to leave," Kate said sadly. "We'll miss everyone here."

"Don't be sad," Bobby said. "You can visit any time!"

"Just follow the footprints to our farm," said Julie.

"We had a great time today!" said Justin.
"We'll come back and visit soon," said Kate.

Justin and Kate sailed away.
They didn't have prizes and
riches. They found something
better. They found the greatest
treasure of all—good friends!

Newton Finds a Family

Illustrated by M. Cambraia Magalhaes

The fair is so much fun! The boys and girls want to live there!

The toy animal prizes do live there! After the fair closes, the toys come to life. They go on the rides. They eat treats.

The toy animals don't live at the fair forever. They hope that a child will win them and take them home.

Each toy animal wants to be part
of a real family.

Newton Frog wants to be part of a real family. But he has lived at the fair longer than the other toys. Newton thinks that no child wants him. He is scared that he will never be picked.

Sadie Elephant, Quint Mouse, and Gabby Rabbit saw Newton crying.

"What's wrong, Newton?" asked Sadie.

"No one wants to win me. I will never be part of a family," Newton cried.

"Please don't cry," sighed Sadie.
"You just have to wait for the right child,"
Gabby said.

"That will never happen," sobbed Newton.

Sadie, Quint, and Gabby took Newton to the fun house. The fun house was Newton's special place. It always made him feel better.

197

"We all look so funny!" laughed Sadie.

"Maybe kids don't want me because I wear glasses!" Newton said.

"Nobody's perfect," Quint said. "I'm small, but that's okay."

"I'm chubby but thats okay, too!"
Sadie said.

"My ears are long but I like them,"
Gabby said.

But Newton still thought that no one
would choose him. He felt sad.

FUN HOUSE →

COTTON CANDY →

← ICE CREAM

Later that day, Marissa Bear saw Newton.

"I just saw Alison Cat with her new family," called Marissa.

"How is she?" Newton asked.

"She is great! She has a new sister," she said.

Alison Cat wasn't perfect. But somebody chose her. Maybe there was hope for Newton. But he still wasn't sure.

One day, Quint was very happy.
"I just saw the perfect child for me!" yelled
Quint. "The boy is very small—just like me!"

"Good luck," said Gabby.

Quint's not perfect, thought Newton. If Quint could find a family maybe he could, too. But he still wasn't sure.

Quint and his new brother were so happy. People chose Alison and Quint. Maybe someone would choose him, too. Newton went back to his game. He waited for a child to come along.

Finally, a little boy came near the game.
Newton was nervous. The boy wore glasses—
just like Newton!

The boy hit the bull's-eye three times in a row.

"I won," the boy shouted. "Which animal should I choose?"

The boy looked at the toys.
Then he said, "I would like that
frog, please."
Newton was so happy!

Newton went home with his new brother. They shared some ice cream. Newton was glad to meet his new family.

The next year, Newton and his family
went to the fair. Newton learned that you
don't have to be perfect. Everyone is
different. Differences make us special!

What's Next, Billy and Jodie?

Illustrated by Becky Radke

Waking Up

Billy opens his arms out wide.

He kicks off the covers.

What's Next?

He builds a palace.

He gets out of bed.

He gets the cookie jar.

Getting Washed

Jodie washes her face.

She brushes her teeth.

What's Next?

She combs her hair.

She sets the table.

She takes a nap.

Eating Breakfast

Billy drinks his juice.

He eats his oatmeal.

What's Next?

He gets out of bed.

He wipes his mouth.

He kicks off the covers.

Playing in the Yard

Billy has a dog. Skippy chews on his bone.

He digs a hole in the ground.

What's Next?

Skippy hides his bone.

Skippy jumps into a car.

Skippy shakes himself dry.

Tea Party

Jodie sets the table.

She seats her dolls.

What's Next?

She brushes her teeth.

She washes her face.

She serves the tea.

Nap Time

Jodie takes off her shoes.

She climbs into bed.

What's Next?

She combs her hair.

She takes a nap.

She sets the table.

Building Blocks

Billy gets his blocks.

He dumps them on the floor.

What's Next?

He builds a palace.

He gets the cookie jar.

He drinks his juice.

Snack Time

Jodie serves the milk.

Billy gets the cookie jar.

What's Next?

Billy builds a palace.

Jodie seats her dolls.

They sit down and eat their snack.

Flying a Kite

Billy takes his kite to the park.

He ties a long tail on his kite.

What's Next?

Billy finds Jodie's friend, Debbie, under the bed.

Billy rides around and around.

Billy watches his kite fly.

Playing Catch

Billy and his best friend, Tommy, put on their baseball mitts.

Tommy throws the ball.

What's Next?

Billy covers his eyes and counts to ten.

Billy ties a long tail on his kite.

Billy catches the ball.

Hide and Seek

Billy closes his eyes and counts to ten.

Debbie hides.

What's Next?

Billy buys a ticket for the ride.

Billy finds Debbie under the bed.

Billy puts on his baseball mitt.

Time for Bed

Skippy is tired.

He gets into his basket.

What's Next?

Billy buys a ticket for the ride.

Billy finds Debbie under the bed.

Billy puts on his baseball mitt.

Time for Bed

Skippy is tired.

He gets into his basket.

He hides his bone.

He goes to sleep.

He gets his leash.

Did you pick the right picture to finish each story?

Waking Up

Billy opens his arms out wide.

He kicks off the covers.

He gets out of bed.

Getting Washed

Jodie washes her face.

She brushes her teeth.

She combs her hair.

Eating Breakfast

Billy drinks his juice.

He eats his oatmeal.

He wipes his mouth.

Playing in the Yard

Billy has a dog. Skippy chews on his bone.

He digs a hole in the ground.

Skippy hides his bone.

Tea Party

Jodie sets the table.

She seats her dolls.

She serves the tea.

Nap Time

Jodie takes off her shoes.

She climbs into bed.

She takes a nap.

Building Blocks

Billy gets his blocks.

He dumps them on the floor.

He builds a palace.

Snack Time

| Jodie serves the milk. | Billy gets the cookie jar. | They sit down and eat their snack. |

Flying a Kite

| Billy takes his kite to the park. | He ties a long tail on his kite. | Billy watches his kite fly. |

Playing Catch

Billy and his best friend, Tommy, put on their baseball mitts.

Tommy throws the ball.

Billy catches the ball.

Hide and Seek

Billy closes his eyes and counts to ten.

Debbie hides.

Billy finds Debbie under the bed.

Time for Bed

Skippy is tired.

He gets into his basket.

He goes to sleep.

Matty's New Neighborhood

Illustrated by Mari Goering

It was moving day. Matty and his family packed up their car. They followed the moving truck to their new neighborhood.

Matty missed his old friends already. He thought about the times he went to the beach with his friends. He wondered if he would make new friends.

At the new house, Matty's mom washed clothes.

"Mom, can we wash my toy animals?" asked Matty. "They want a fresh start here, too."

Matty thought about his new
neighborhood. He was afraid again.
He told his toy dog, Buddy, all about it.
   "What if the kids don't like me?"
asked Matty.

Matty's old friends didn't forget about him. Kayla wrote a letter to Matty every day. Matty wrote back as soon as he got each letter.

Matty's little sister, Lisa, liked their new home. She unpacked. She put everything in a special place.

Matty was afraid of the first day
in his new school.
"Have a good day, Matty," said his dad.

At school, Matty's class went to the art room. Some children drew pictures. Some worked with clay. Matty just watched. He was too shy to play with them.

Matty didn't like his new school. He felt lonely. He felt sad. No one played with Matty all morning.

The next day, Matty's teacher helped him learn all of the kids' names.

"The other kids have to get to know you. You are new to them, too," said the teacher.

Matty felt better.

Lisa was having a good time in her new class. She met a boy named Richard. Lisa liked her new school.

259

Soon Matty began to feel better about his new school. He felt better about his new neighborhood, too. He walked to school with his new friends.

Matty and his new friends played hide-and-seek. Matty didn't feel like the new kid on the block anymore!

One day Matty heard
his dog barking. He saw
someone he had never seen
before.

"I hit my ball over the fence. I came
to get it," said the boy.

"Are you new around here?" asked Matty.

"I just moved in next door. My name is Jerry," said the boy.

"My name's Matty and this is my dog, Red," said Matty.

Jerry liked Red. Jerry liked Matty. Jerry hoped he was going to like his new neighborhood.

The next day Jerry went to the playground. He didn't see Matty. Jerry hoped that he would make friends with the children. It was easy to make friends with Matty.

Matty ate lunch with his friend
Stephanie and her mom. He told
them about Jerry.

"Let's ask him to come to my
birthday party," said Stephanie.

Matty knew how it felt to be the
new kid. He wanted Jerry to meet
his new friends.

271

Stephanie's birthday party was fun. Jerry
was glad Matty asked him to the party.

Matty was glad that Jerry
felt good. It was nice to
see him make new friends.

Matty and Jerry were both glad to have new friends. Matty didn't miss his old neighborhood so much anymore. He learned that meeting new people and going to new places can be fun.

Jack's Summer at Camp

Illustrated by Sally Masteller

This was Jack's first time away at summer camp. There would be fun things to do! He would make new friends!

Max and Nicky went fishing. Jack decided to play a trick. Jack crept up behind Jessie. Jack scared her with a worm.

Jessie was angry with Jack.

"That wasn't a nice thing to do," said Jessie.

She was not sure if she wanted to be his friend.

The children got their turtles ready for a race. Jessie and Max were having fun. Max's turtle was in the lead!

"I'll fix that," Jack said with a grin.

Max's turtle was near the finish line. Jack took Max's turtle out of the race. Now Jack's turtle could win.

"It is not fun to play with you," said Max.

"We may not be the best, but we have fun," said Nicky.

One day, the kids went to plant flowers in the garden. Suddenly, Jack ran ahead.

"I'm going to be first!" Jack called. "I will get the best spot."

Soon, no one asked Jack to play.

"Don't you want me on your team?" asked Jack.

"No," Nicky said. "We have enough players."

Jack felt lonely. Nobody wanted to play
with him. They were all having fun.

One day the kids found a can.
"I wonder what is inside," Max said.
"I don't know," Jessie said. "I'll open it and find out."
"No," Jack snapped. "I'll open it."

Jack opened the can. He got a surprise! Inside the can were creepy worms. Everyone laughed.

"Hey, you tricked me!" cried Jack.

"You wanted the can!" Nicky told him.

Jack was so angry. He said that he didn't care. He would have fun playing by himself.

Later that day, Jessie's cat, Jade, fell into a hole.

"Oh no," cried Jessie. "I can't reach Jade!"

"I have a plan," Jack called.

Jack saved Jade.

"Thank you. That was nice," said Jessie.
"Would you like to play?"

"You're not so bad when you're being nice," Max said.

"I'm sorry that I was mean," Jack said. "I thought that you would like me if I could do everything well."

"Just be yourself. Everyone will like you," Jessie said.

START

298

At the next turtle race, Jack did not trick them. His turtle was the slowest. Max's turtle came in first place.

"Great job, Max!" Jack said. He really meant it.

FINISH

They went to the garden to plant more flowers. Jack ran ahead. He saved the best spot. But this time it wasn't for himself.

"Come on," called Jack. "I saved a great spot for you!"

Jack took turns with the others. He didn't keep the best toys for himself.

"Here Jack, it's your turn," Nicky said.

"Thanks," said Jack.

Jack had a great summer at camp. He learned how to make friends. He learned how to share. He learned how to be himself. "I can't wait for next summer!" said Jack.